Wonderful You

A NOTE FROM THE AUTHOR

Every adoption story is different, but many of them share one thing—a sense of destiny. When a child who needs a family is joined with a family that needs a child, it can seem like fate. I'll never forget the first time I saw my adoptive daughter. She was perfectly formed and full of life. When I extended my little finger toward her, she gripped it. That was it. I was hers forever. Since then our life together has been a wonderful adventure. I wanted to celebrate this adventure, and the birth mother who made it all possible—from her courageous journey to find a loving home to the moment we became the family I believe we were always meant to be.

Every family story is a fairy tale. This is ours.

Visit us on the Web! randomhousekids.com

Educators and librarians, for a variety of teaching tools, visit us at RHTeachersLibrarians.com

Library of Congress Cataloging-in-Publication Data is available upon request.

ISBN 978-0-553-51001-0 (trade) — ISBN 978-0-553-51003-4 (lib. bdg.) — ISBN 978-0-553-51002-7 (ebook)

MANUFACTURED IN CHINA
10 9 8 7 6 5 4 3 2 1
First Edition

Wonderful You

An Adoption Story

by Lauren McLaughlin

illustrated by Meilo So

Random House 🏠 New York

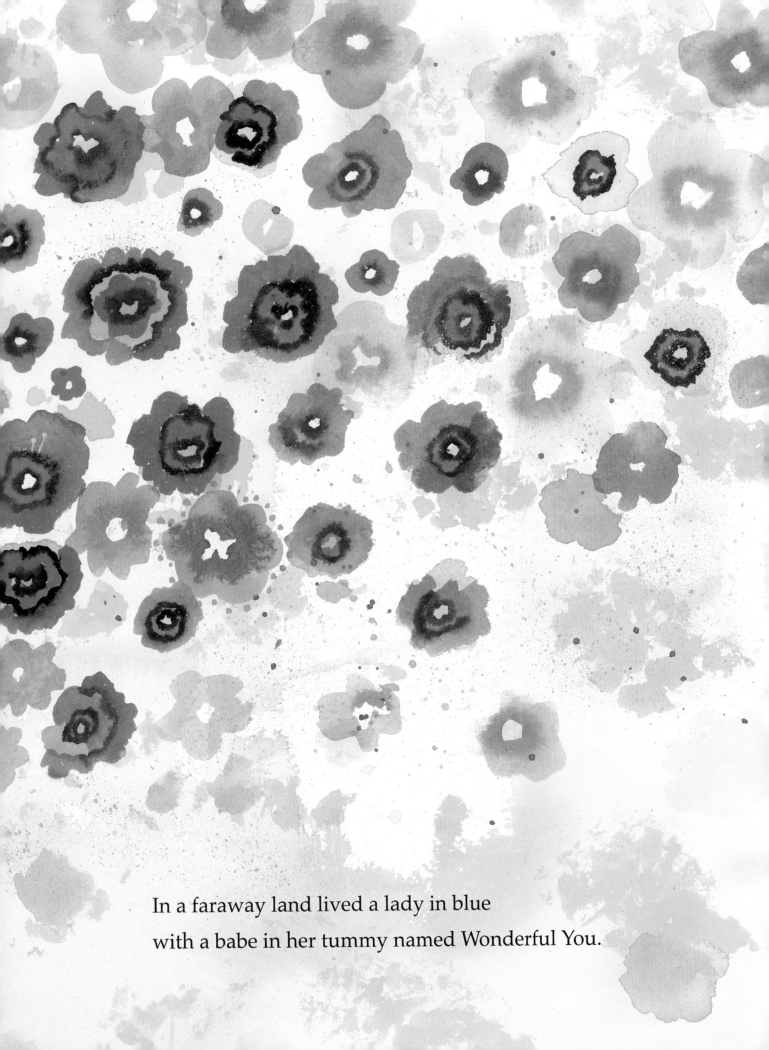

In a faraway land lived a lady in blue
with a babe in her tummy named Wonderful You.

She looked north. She looked south. She traveled the world, asking, "Who'll be the parents of this beautiful girl?

"I will sail by the moon and the stars till I find
a home for my girl that is loving and kind,
with a soft, cushioned bed and a teddy named Boo.

"Nothing less than the best for Wonderful You."

Then the lady in blue spied your father and me
in our home in the dunes by the sky-blue sea.

"Can it be? Can it be?" asked your father and me.
"Is she looking for us? Is it time finally?

"We have waited so long for the lady in blue,
but here she is now with Wonderful You.
We've fixed up your crib and found you a teddy.
We already love you. We promise we're ready."

The lady in blue looked us over some more.
She liked what she saw, but she had to be sure.

"Will you love her," she asked, "every morning and night?
And all times between, whether rainy or bright?"

"We will hug her and kiss her and tickle her too.
Forever and always, our Wonderful You."

Then the lady in blue put your small hand in mine.
"You're the ones I've traveled the whole world to find."
Back to her faraway land did she roam,
knowing that you were finally home.

And here you are now with your teddy named Boo,
forever and always our Wonderful You.

We were made for each other, as families are,

whether big ones or small ones, from near or from far . . .

each one, in its way, a story unfolding
of laughter and teardrops and arms made for holding.

But you are the magic in this fairy tale.
Adventure awaits. Come, let's set sail!

There is so much to do and to see, little one.

There'll be crawling,
then walking,
then one day you'll run.

There'll be birthdays and school days and trips to the zoo.

We'll build towers and snowmen and palaces too.

And one thing you'll know every morning and night,
when we come wake you up, when we put out the light:

As the shore hugs the sea, no matter the tide,
your mommy and daddy will be at your side.

All this and more we promise to you,
our magical, beautiful Wonderful You.